The Nettleham Gentlemen's Club

The Nettleham Gentlemen's Club

CHARLES WILLIAM JOHNS

RESOURCE *Publications* • Eugene, Oregon

THE NETTLEHAM GENTLEMEN'S CLUB

Resource Publications
An Imprint of Wipf and Stock Publishers
199 W. 8th Ave., Suite 3
Eugene, OR 97401

www.wipfandstock.com

PAPERBACK ISBN: 978-1-6667-1640-5
HARDCOVER ISBN: 978-1-6667-1641-2
EBOOK ISBN: 978-1-6667-1642-9

JULY 15, 2021

This book is dedicated to my angelic mother, Belinda

I wrote the entirety of this book sipping champagne (I swear to God!).
Perhaps a few Campari's. Maybe some wine.
Well, anything lying around the house really.

Contents

Preface

Throughout the annals of the terrestrial animal kingdom it has been noted that there is at least one common denominator shared between the species homo erectus and homo sapien: the act of assigning *mystery* to things. This mystery is ascribed to things that *they* previously did no*t*, or presently do not, have knowledge of. First, they acquired the nerve to pester the whole animal kingdom (they were hungry). You know what they say: "If at first you don't succeed, pry, pry again!"

Then it was all that awful business with the "hot burny" stuff called *fire*. Three million years of trial and error (and lots of laughing) and what for? I say we should all keep ourselves to ourselves. It's a matter of relativity really; would Clarence have his beloved yacht with its uranium keel if the nuclear bomb were never invented ? Would Victor have burnt his bungalow down in a freak fried bacon accident if those pesky fur-clad chaps hadn't mastered the art of rubbing two sticks together? It is not only cats that bear the brunt of this curiosity business. To hell with mystery!

In our contemporary times we have a less threatening kind of mystery: people want to *learn* about everything. To recite every Shakespeare sonnet, to travel the world, to swim with dolphins, to know the difference between Focaccia and Ciabatta bread. If they are not busy chasing such *experiences*, then they will be at home continually questioning themselves, their appearance to others, and the meaning of their lives. There is also a small demographic (philosophers) wishing to spend all its time pondering existence *itself*, as if it were something we could just pick up and analyse, or some futile, cosmic magic trick without any real finale. Some even search for a Platonic realm, which apparently dwells deep within or behind the kingdom of normal human appearance and experience.

This does *not* sit well with the members of the Nettleham Gentlemen's Club.

I wonder what the Platonic truth of a cheese and pickle sandwich for sale at the Nettleham Village Tea Shop would be? If there, indeed, were some necessary exactitude or essence to the sandwich, would it be latent in the cheese or the pickle, or the bread slices? I would argue, on behalf of the Nettleham Gentlemen's Club, that appetite would vanquish any desire for truth (or mystery for that matter); one cannot have their sandwich and eat it, can they?

If you ever find yourself ruminating upon a pedestrian signpost, asking those very same *metaphysical* questions pertaining to the meaning and *being* of this object, then just remember: if you ponder for too long, you may get *lost in truth* . . . and you'll be late to the pub.

Charles William Johns

01/01/2021

INTRODUCTION

IT IS THE YEAR two thousand and twenty one and we are in the throes of utterly dispensing with *English taste* even though our political circumstances profess the opposite. These may be troubling times but not for the majority of those living in Nettleham. A large number of its inhabitants are living off their well-deserved pensions, others simply wish to reside outside the hustle and bustle of the city (Lincoln), some fall in love with the village and want to have its babies. It is with utter affection that I must confess many of these Nettlehamites have lost, long ago, any sparkle of circadian rhythm. When I take my three p.m. stroll through the village, I peer through many of its residential windows. I am presented with faces positioned upwards towards their ceilings. At first, I wonder what they must be looking at, but through closer inspection I find that their eyes are closed; they are slumped on their sofas like long forgotten shipwrecks buried in the depths of the sea. If one is incredulous to their state of wakefulness, one must only look closer at the drool accompanying them and stretching from the lower lip to the collar bone. If one is strangely inclined to do so, one can imagine that the drool is still warm, like butter oozing through the holes of a hot crumpet.

When I take my walks, I pay special attention to every entity I encounter. I particularly enjoy objects manufactured over the last two hundred years: bus stops, letter boxes, lamp posts, benches with memorials engraved in them, baffle and kissing gates, etc. Of course, there are many Saxon and Mediaeval remnants scattered throughout the village, yet the Victorian Era always enlivens me for some reason.

On one of these walks I came across the Nettleham Gentlemen's Club. I followed trails of grass, mud, and dew, much as if I were a dog roaming along with my owner. I tend to look at my feet when I walk if I have not already been distracted by something or other above waist level, however, I remember someone telling me this was an uncultivated thing to do as one may suspect that you were searching for money or cigarette ends (I am prone to agree). Anyway, I came across what I thought to be a cul de sac towards the end of Greenfields Road. Intrigued by dead ends in general I followed it to its *terminus ad quem* to find a great expanse of land before me. It couldn't have been later than four p.m. yet I had to review this assumption after seeing nine men rolling about on a lawn, braces broken, buttons popped, collars unfurled, panting with prosecco glasses in their hands. On witnessing their impressive display, I couldn't help but think of the seventh chapter of the Gospel of Matthew in the New Testament:

> To come to eternal happiness, do not follow the great number and multitude of men but join thyself to the small sanctified flock.

It was my ambition to do so, with these strange Epicurean men. Oh, and it turned out Mrs. Bramble had dropped her shopping list and the wind took to blowing it about a bit. The nine gentlemen were determined to retrieve such an invaluable object and outmanoeuvre the west wind of Zephyrus. Their effort was equivalent to Mrs. Bramble's despair; it would take Rebecca Bramble another half an hour to re-write the list (she had arthritis). Jeffrey Bramble was at the forefront of the hustle, not because he was compelled by unconditional love and support for his wife, Rebecca

Bramble (in sickness and in health . . . and in catching things that fly off in the wind), but because he had spent the whole morning convincing Rebecca that his help in yesterday's charity raffle made him deserving of carrot cake. This addition was hesitantly added to the list by Rebecca, and Jeffrey knew that if he failed to procure the original list he may have to say goodbye to that almost fortuitous carrot beauty.

The chance encounter was how I first got to meet all nine members of the Club. It is now almost exactly a year since they took me under their wing. Unfortunately, it is also time for me to leave them (if anything I was only ever a temporary member; there will be no statues made of me when all is said and done). I walked away from Mulsanne Park for the last time, leaving everything behind: the Pavilion where we drank, played cards . . . and drank. The Nettleham Bowls Club, the cricket pitch, the 'club bench' we all piled upon during summer (eternally covered in cherry blossom). The tennis courts with their side lines, which Mrs Bramble demanded us to walk on as steadily as possible – as if victims on a pirates' plank – to discern how many snifters we had executed that day.

What follows is as accurate an account of those men as lies in my capacity to give. I have never been awfully interested in 'grand narratives', as Jeffrey once said – most people have had neither the luxury nor the tragedy of being involved in such stories. We do not live in a time of Barabases, of Caligulas (or would that be Caliguli?), of Romeos and Juliets. We instead live in an epoch where man can only sincerely talk of the minutiae, their immediate environment, and those passing people and places that stir the heart and remind them of their place in the great chain of being.

I walk home, melancholic and alone, as if I were an exhausted child leaving school after a dreary day of lessons. The reality of work, children, and social obligations demand me to break from the 'salad days' of The Nettleham Gentlemen's Club, but I will never forget it. As I have said somewhere before: things must end before they can be remembered.

Victor Drake

Victor Drake is an obese man, so much so that the rest of the Gentlemen's Club describe him as "Humpty Dumpty's fat egg brother." His favourite drink (Victor's, not the victim of the wall incident) is a gin rickey and his favourite food is cocktail sausages. If any of the other members of The Gentlemen's Club had ever said something unfavourable towards him accidentally (on purpose) that caused Victor considerable distress, then sausages and gin would be flung at him from every angle as quickly as you could say "Jack Robinson" (or as the Gentlemen's Club adopted: as soon as you could say "a pig's curly whirly").

His favourite colour is green, his favourite egg is poached, and upon visiting a zoo, he is remembered for saying, "They're alive!" He is by far the best backgammon player of the bunch but when it comes to more physically demanding games such as tennis and cricket, he likes to remind us that his big toe was severely compromised due to his time in the Second Armoured Division (yes, he won't hesitate to tell you he has seen the Sphinx and that it is "ghastly"). This 'injury' does not stop him from shouting obscenities whenever the county cricket team plays on home turf at

Nettleham. Club favourites include "Get over there, you dosser!", "Just bosh it!", "Stop picking your nose!" and "Cocktail sausages?"

One of my favourite instances was when Victor decided to impart to us his specialist knowledge of "popping". Most mornings he would "pop" to the Post Office to send his younger brother the newest edition of themed stamps – stamps that, in his own words, "capture, commemorate and celebrate the nation's passions." Victor's brother George lived in France you see, and this had been a thoroughly reciprocated pasttime since both discovered foreign stamps on their military travels. Victor would send George new sets of stamps whenever they were available and George kindly followed suit.

On a cold December in Nettleham at the Pavilion, whilst figures of The Gentlemen's Club rolled their sixth or seventh cigarette, Victor spontaneously decided to explicate his "popping" knowledge upon his most trusted companions.

...

"I pop to the Nettleham Post Office most days. To 'pop' would suggest a quick, easy, and light-hearted visit. I cannot imagine someone popping to Costa Rica, The Holocaust Memorial Museum, or to prison. The conditions for popping are short distances and at least two or three minutes of spare time (some popping duration).

You can start a pop and end exhausted from a laborious journey. A pop is always the ideal but rarely the reality. In my experience, although popping is light-hearted (for the reasons above), one almost always has a job in mind when one pops. I would 'pop' to the library to return a book, but I probably wouldn't pop to the library to decide which book I should like to take away with me. I don't think you can pop to a church (unless you are a member of the clergy and have forgotten your umbrella). People sometimes try and use the word 'pop' to cover up contrary desires; I sometimes 'pop' to the pub but I intend nothing of the sort. "Darling, I really must pop to the pub. There is a full pint of beer that must be emptied crucially and swiftly"

I give the illusion of popping to the pub, so my spouse, friend, or family member will rest assured I will not be long, but really, there will be no popping. I am unpoppable in such situations.

So, I pop to the Post Office. Or do I 'nip'? To nip is to do something quickly of course. I could 'nip' into the Post Office quickly, but I feel the word pop has more breadth to it.

I am not in a rush, I am popping (who knows for how long?). I will enjoy popping to the Post Office; there is no need to get it out of the way or to do something before it is too late. That would be to nip; to nip something in the bud before it gets worse. I am not nipping the way a pet hamster may nip its owner. I will not nip into the Post Office as if I were attacking it.

Don't even get me started with 'shooting'! No, I am not shooting off anywhere! I am not a rocket!

What a strange world we live in, eh chaps? Is there still room for a pop? Anyone got some cocktail sausages?"

CLARENCE CONSTABLE

CLARENCE CONSTABLE IS A retired farmer – an honorary member of The Nettleham Gentlemen's Club since 1982. Awarded largest marrow at the Nettleham Marrow contest of '98. So large, he likes to boast, that one lady called it "an eyesore." His oeuvre of marrow jokes consists of the now famous (Nettleham famous) witticism:

> "My friend needed a marrow transplant and we found a perfect match in Nettleham. The operation took place and was a great success. My thanks go out to Clarence Constable, Marrow Donor."

Clarence lost his wife in 91 but attests that "she would have hated the twenty-first century . . . some people get all the fun." He is an avid smoker and takes a silver cigarette case with him wherever he goes. If others display their cigarettes in the manufacturer's box, he often looks at them and remarks, "Did you leave your case at home?" He reminds us that, "Princess Margaret wouldn't be caught dead without her cigarette case."

Clarence enjoys Purcell and Grainger. He hates Beethoven (for obvious reasons) and accuses Elgar of trying to be "too German." Clarence hates most things and likes even less.

His Achilles heel is cheese and he will never let us forget his sordid experience at a local supermarket:

…

"I walk into this supermarket (I am yet to know what is 'super' about it) and immediately I encounter these automatic doors. Well, first, I am in no need of assistance when it comes to entering or exiting buildings thank you. I am not one of these people on drugs who always plays video games and cannot do anything for themselves don't you know. I've been opening doors since I was five years old. I even take the responsibility of opening them for other people.

"Anyway, I have to manoeuvre around the 'special offers' before I can even get sight of the supermarket aisles. First of all, it is far too busy; why must they all come when I am visiting? There should be a rota. I do not bother with those obscene trolleys (apparently you must pay for them). Instead, I allow myself the smallest shopping basket and head to the cheese counter. I must tell you that there are *two* cheese sections. I do not trust the cheese section in the supermarket aisle (I do not know how much I am getting if it has not been cut to *my* measurements). I march to the *official* cheese counter and I cannot complain – there are many cheeses. It would take a lifetime to go through all their cheeses. Who knew the Africans and the Middle East had time to make cheese? Amongst all the poverty and wars, some old chap has the wherewithal to make the good stuff?! I decide on my two cheeses: a Shropshire Blue and a Celtic Gold. I am in the moment of a comestible transaction yet there is no one to be seen. Someone has defected and is cutting ham. I do not know how long to wait but I can see the cheese I desire, it is right there, so it cannot take longer than a gentle nudge and a swift procurement. When the deceitful cheese lady finally notices me, she asks me what my number is. I start to recite my telephone number to her, but she does not look impressed. I am instructed to get a number token from the far side of the counter. I ask myself why I must do this. I am obviously the only person at the cheese counter, and I wish for some

Shropshire Blue and some Celtic Gold. I say to her "Shropshire Blue and Celtic Gold please." She appears to ignore me. I make my way to this unknown place where some kind of amusement park ticket machine can be found. I pluck a ticket out of the machine (regrettably I must have taken about six tickets). I immediately fall for this elaborate ploy; even if I die here on this spot, people will attest that I have, indeed, got my ticket. If, in the Afterlife, I am allowed the one vice of some Shropshire Blue and Celtic Gold, there will be no one who can deny my right, through the medium of a token, to such cheeses."

...

This soliloquy lasted for more than an hour and the words "Shropshire Blue" and "Celtic Gold" must have made an appearance more than fifty times. All in all, Clarence is a good sort but we must never ask him to go to the supermarket again.

Cecil Cluck

Cecil arrived at the Club shortly before I did. Apparently, about a year ago, he introduced himself to one of the Club members, asked them for the time, and has since never left. The name Cluck is of Scottish descent (he likes to remind us of this when we get out the whiskey). Cecil is unfortunately etymologically linked to the word 'blind' (from the Roman clan name 'Caecilius') and his surname, Cluck, I imagine, has something to do with the low, interrupted noise a chicken makes. I guess you could say in a sort of roundabout way that Cecil Cluck means 'blind chicken.'

We often substitute the 'f' word for cluck – "Cluck off, you old barmy toad," "cluuuuuuckingggg hell!" or my personal favourite, "Where the cluck is Cluck?" (Things of that nature.)

Sometimes we are all at the Pavilion, sans Cecil, having a whale of a time, cards being shuffled, the usual bouquet of abuse spilling out upon everyone, and we take a moment to ask ourselves why we are having such a lovely time (a bit philosophical and silly really) and we all come to the conclusion that it is because Cecil is not here, and just like that, he enters the room. He reminds me of that 3 o'clock headache in the afternoon, which confesses to the last tipple of port you really should not have had the prior evening;

you must acknowledge it, yet you do everything in your power to vanquish its existence and effects.

Cecil has a few supernatural talents, however. He can sleep almost anywhere. Many times I have turned my head to see where the cluck Cecil has got to and he has been sprawled out across a set of chairs (you can almost imagine his thinking, *Yes three chairs ought to do it*). When he is not reclined in this cocoon-like state, he may still be unconscious *somewhere,* draped over one of the tennis nets looking like a pair of soggy trousers on a washing line. Curled up under the games table like a trusty old dog at a pub. At one point we all thought he had mastered the art of levitation, however, upon closer inspection, we realised he had acquired Mrs. Brambles's ironing board, set it up, and laid himself out rather miraculously – distributing all of his weight evenly without the slightest bit of tipping. Jeffrey said he looked like a sacrifice to the gods.

The incredible thing is that when you confront him about his creative narcolepsy, he rejoices in it. In his own words.

...

"Well yes, there are many ways to sleep, possibly more ways to sleep than be awake I imagine. I tend to go for the good old-fashioned lie-down first: flat back, occipital bun fully supported, feet pointing up and turned out slightly with arms to the side. If one's arms are being a little mischievous, then the classic 'hammock stance' will suffice: arms above the head, starfish sleeping yet connected by the superior 'hand-clasping' action. Failing that you can always opt for what I call the 'one-armed front crawl'. You sort of fling your right arm out in front of you as if you were Superman preparing for flight and then nuzzle your ear into your arm (can one nuzzle with an ear?).

"I have always found it is more the *location* of sleep rather than the technique. Shakespeare famously said that "all the world's a stage". Well, such a stage is teeming with soporific spots. Absolutely nothing wrong with sleeping in a bush if one is prepared for the initial spikey entrance. I have once favoured a lamppost for such inactivity; the trick is to put both arms out as if one is about to be walloped by a double-decker bus. Leaning on the old trunk with both palms stretched out (preferably kneeling), one is almost taken over by a saintly attitude: *In peace I will lie down and sleep, for you alone, Lord, make me dwell in safety* (Psalm 24:8).

"Whenever one is awake, one must also be in the process of gradually sleeping; impending tiredness is a phenomenon that never leaves me, especially after the old afternoon thirst quencher at the Pavilion. Sometimes, during a lively evening at The Gentlemen's Club, my wife encourages me to catch forty winks, or at least half a dozen, and she is quite right! What a maternal angel she is. I bid everyone farewell and add that I will only be inches away.

"I imagine that the Afterlife should be quite a pleasant place for me. I hope everyone hasn't taken all the best spots! I'm not sure if I could even make the journey without a harmless snooze. I imagine I might create a pact with Thomas before going in. I could ask him some ambiguous question with the hope that he might reply in some long-winded fashion. I'll ask him what all that doubting business of his was about. He would then go off on some mad soliloquy and I just might gather a few somnolent moments at the Pearly Gates."

JEFFREY BRAMBLE

JEFFREY BRAMBLE IS, WITHOUT proper title, the King of The Nettleham Gentlemen's Club, the glue that keeps it all together. He and his wife Rebecca organise every get-together (although everyone just turns up sometime between 9 - 12 am nowadays). Rebecca, although not a gentleman, is seen as the sole Lady of the Club, a lady held in the highest esteem. If asked what specific function Rebecca brings to the Club, she would answer, "To let the boys get on with whatever they wish to get on with . . . as long as it is without malice . . . and they would starve without me." This is indeed true. Once Rebecca had to visit her sister in Devon for a few days and Clarence took charge of the catering duties. On returning from her visit to Devon, Rebecca entered The Gentlemen's Club to find precisely thirty-three empty chocolate Advent calendars (it was the middle of March!), accompanied by nine men sipping the dregs of Victor's 1998 'prize brew'. Not to worry though – Clarence had scrambled a dozen eggs the day before and put them in the refrigerator to make egg and cress sandwiches.

Lady Rebecca Bramble looked straight towards her spouse in search for answers . . . and signs of life. Jeffrey replied:

. . .

"Look darling. The chocolates were a present. What I mean to say is they *presented* themselves to us in a skip just across the road from the Pavilion. We tried to ration ourselves to one a day, you know, to keep up with the spirit of the whole thing, but Cecil couldn't figure out how many days had passed due to his narcolepsy, so we thought, out of solidarity, that we should all be on the same page . . . as it were. I think one day about thirty days passed; it was a real phenomenon! Not to worry. We opened them chronologically. Victor has saved you the 25th window, so you don't feel left out. I can't say the same for Charles though; he may or may not have tried to eat the calendar itself, to get rid of the evidence . . . as it were.

"You know, there were times we barely realised you had left in the first place, what with attending to our chocolates . . . and Victor's home brew. You know, I really think it needed that time to properly get its flavour, to ferment . . . as it were. We had our very own system of self-sufficiency; over the last few days we have even been calling each other *comrade*!

Now, I would ask you *not* to look at the cabbage patch behind the church. Some nasty rabbits have taken to it and it doesn't look pretty. At first glance the bites do seem to look human sized, but it's because they were all going for the same piece. It's an accumulation of smaller bites you see. If there are any remnants of cabbage in the Pavilion this is because they tried to attack us too! Now, it is Charles' opinion that rabbits have rabies. Whether this is a case of mere alliteration, or something very real and dangerous, is only secondary to the question – will the rabbits steal our chocolates? Yes, Charles had already come up with the suggestion that it is mid-March and the rabbits may have thought we had forgotten all about Easter and were instead gluttonously easing into yet another chocolate Christmas month. Victor reminded us that we were weeks away from easter so theoretically there has been no festive taboo, chocolate or otherwise. I don't see why we can't have both, do you? Anyway, hygienically the last few days have been a pickle; Cecil is just waiting for the dishwasher to beep to put in another pile of clothes."

Sydney Black

Sydney Black likes to lick the spoon when Mrs. Bramble makes peanut butter and marmite sandwiches. He likes to sport – and keep well-groomed – a pencil moustache. He thinks that ham is made from hamster meat and he won't go near mince pies. Peanut butter is made of peas (which is fine) and marmite is . . . well it's a condiment. Walking underneath a ladder is just plain dangerous, let alone bad luck, and snow is not frozen rain but little bits of the North Pole that only come out when it's Christmas (he has obviously never been to Canada).

Sydney was divorced in 1981 and before he started hanging around The Gentlemen's Club, he used to stay at home building and painting model airplanes. Since he caught wind that his ex-wife had died a few years ago, he has been obsessed with death. In his very own words: "When I am not eating peanut butter and marmite sandwiches, I am thinking of death." Jeffrey wasn't sure if he should be worried or not, but then we all found out what *type* of relationship Sydney had to the Grim Reaper. That's when we knew for sure he was a maniac but not a lost cause. In his own words:

. . .

"Well, the way I see it is that you spend most of your life dying, and afterwards you're dead for a very long time, maybe forever, so *where* you get buried is of the utmost importance, tantamount to where you live. *Victor* thinks that he will get into the Nettleham church graveyard because he knows the vicar, but I pray every day and I know for a fact that the others only do on Sundays . . . so I have the advantage. *Jeffrey* keeps the apple tree from falling next to the church, so I bet he thinks he's *in* whatever the weather. And they won't stop *Rebecca* from joining in if *Jeffrey* goes. *Charles* thinks he's going smack bang in the middle because once, when his pet goldfish died, he buried it in his back garden and read a William Blake poem. *Clarence* is surer than any of them because his favourite thing is cheese and it rhymes with Jesus, or at least the plural (. . . of cheese that is). Bertram dismisses the question because he thinks it's bonkers to talk about death amongst all this wonderful life and merriment . . . so every time we discuss it he asks us to pass him the Aperol and goes off to check the Orchids.

"*Henry* has a theory that there are only nine spaces left in the church graveyard, so one of us will have to stay in the Pavilion, unless Jeffrey and Rebecca bunk up with one another. Maybe Victor and Clarence might opt for sharing a coffin . . . they're always telling each other to "go to hell!" If Victor could just lose some weight, then we may gain an additional three or four spaces.

"If Henry *is* right, then a plan must be drawn up! I'll have to try and make the rest of the Club live longer somehow. Perhaps I could give myself the largest pouring of brandy in the evenings to relieve the chaps of any significant liver dysfunctions. Perhaps I could take up smoking and ask for copious amounts of tobacco from the rest of the gang, reducing their chances of lung cancer. Or am I going about this the wrong way? Is it I that must up the ante myself, as a sort of willing sacrifice? A generous helping of pork scratchings, donuts, and beer for breakfast, followed by chips and an illegal substance of some kind for lunch, and then I could possibly just stick my head down the lavatory whenever I wished to quench my thirst. If such a task is possible, then I must also refrain from any type of exercise and I may even have to give up walking all together. Maybe they could push me about in a wheelchair with a catheter full of Absinthe.

"Come to think of it, maybe I'll just keep an eager eye on Victor over the next few years; he's bound to spontaneously combust at some point."

If you ever find yourself ruminating upon a signpost, asking those very same
metaphysical questions pertaining to the meaning and being of this object,
then just remember: if you ponder for too long, you may get lost in truth
. . . and you'll be late to the pub.

These may be troubling times but not for the majority of those living in Nettleham. A large number of its inhabitants are living off their well-deserved pensions, others simply wish to reside outside the hustle and bustle of the city (Lincoln), some fall in love with the village and want to have its babies.

Victor thinks that he will get into the Nettleham church graveyard because he knows the vicar, but I pray every day and I know for a fact that the others only do on Sundays . . . so I have the advantage. Jeffrey keeps the apple tree from falling next to the church, so I bet he thinks he's in whatever the weather.

I pop to the Nettleham Post Office most days. To 'pop' would suggest a quick, easy, and light-hearted visit. I cannot imagine someone popping to Costa Rica, The Holocaust Memorial Museum, or to prison. The conditions for popping are short distances and at least two or three minutes of spare time (some popping duration).

Once Charles forgot where the Pavilion was and spent the evening playing cards with the Nettleham Weight Watchers group sipping tomato and herb bulgur wheat soup followed by flourless carrot cake flapjacks.
He keeps requesting that we should all do it again sometime.

People sometimes try and use the word 'pop' to cover up contrary desires;
I sometimes 'pop' to the pub but I intend nothing of the sort.
I am unpoppable in such situations.

Well yes, there are many ways to sleep, possibly more ways to sleep than be awake I imagine. I tend to go for the good old-fashioned lie-down first: flat back, occipital bun fully supported, feet pointing up and turned out slightly with arms to the side.

Do not serve any amount of fish or chips to Mr Charles Dumbridge . . .
as he is absolutely crackers . . . and we don't sell those here.

The smell of freshly cut grass originating from the Nettleham F.C football pitch. The colour and taste of Kalamata olives mixed with broken feta cheese prepared and brought outside by Rebecca Bramble just after 5:00 p.m.

This 'injury' does not stop him from shouting obscenities whenever the county cricket team plays on home turf at Nettleham. Club favourites include "Get over there, you dosser!", "Just bosh it!", "Stop picking your nose!" and "Cocktail sausages?

The tennis courts with their side lines, which Mrs Bramble demanded us to walk on as steadily as possible – as if victims on a pirates' plank – to discern how many snifters we had executed that day.

I walked away from Mulsanne Park for the last time, leaving everything behind: the Pavilion where we drank, played cards . . . and drank.

The Nettleham Bowls Club, the cricket pitch, and the 'club bench' we all piled upon during summer (eternally covered in cherry blossom).

It is now almost exactly a year since they took me under their wing. Unfortunately, it is also time for me to leave them (if anything I was only ever a temporary member; there will be no statues made of me when all is said and done).

Charles Dumbridge

Charles Dumbridge is severely and pleasantly lost in his own world. He has never worked a single day in his life apart from once when he delivered a parcel next-door-but-one that was wrongly sent to his own address. He can't quite fathom why benches aren't accompanied with cushions, and whenever we ask him to procure some pitted olives from the local shop he always comes back an hour later with a jar of olives stuck in his underarm (the 'axilla' if you wish for the proper anatomical term). His favourite, very own signature joke, is as follows:

> Knock, knock
> Who's there?
> Pneumonoultramicroscopicsilicovolcanoconiosis.

...

No one has quite made it to the end of the joke yet.

Most of the time Charles can't even get through the delivery.

Once Charles forgot where the Pavilion was and spent the evening playing cards with the Nettleham Weight Watchers group sipping tomato and herb bulgur wheat soup followed by flourless carrot cake flapjacks. He keeps requesting that we should all do it again sometime.

Charles isn't really a natural storyteller (or joke teller) but he will take the time to tell you exactly what he does and does not like. Here is a list compiled by Charles himself.

Charles's dislikes:

Eggs, the white bits of eggs, the yellow bits of eggs, eggs generally speaking, taps that drip even when they have been turned off, wine that is less than 12% in alcoholic content, playing cards that are not laminated, menthol cigarettes, people who have words on their clothes, middle partings, papercuts, paper, cuts, meringue (!), Bertram Bloom, any time before 11:00 a.m., waking up early, horses, paintings with horses in them, dinosaurs, fireworks, mirrors, bowties, television, people who exercise, exercising, books that are longer than 100 pages, buying pitted olives, the second half of a piano, any high sounds, sunsets, men who wear jewellery, newspapers, Beethoven, rabbits, Bertram Bloom, that strange spinning sensation after too many snifters, warm bread that is passing itself off as toast, the colour red, jigsaw puzzles with pieces missing, chewing gum, Shropshire Blue and Celtic Gold, Velcro, people who say "ostensibly," anything that lives underwater, children, car parks, dimmer switches and Bertram Bloom.

Charles's likes:

Anchovies, parmesan, big pieces of salt on food, the colour green, Purcell, ballet, burnt toast, lemon juice, ready salted crisps, Scotland, pocket tissues, candles, black and white films, autumn, the Nettleham Church bells ... and chips

About chips, Charles is possibly the only Nettlehamite who has been banned from entering Franky's Fish Bar on account of his "mischievous and sarcastic behaviour." This is not how Charles would put it, however. This is what he had to say about it when pushed on the subject:

. . .

"Well, I went to the fish and chip shop because everyone wanted fish and chips, that's simple enough. It should have been an in and out job; me with my fish and chips, and Franky with his hard-earned cash. It should have been a breezy transaction . . . but Franky is a stupid idiot!

So, I went in there, joined the queue and waited patiently, repositioning my hat several times. The chap in front of me received his hot paper bag of chips, so I said to Franky, 'I'll have 51 chips please.' Franky looked at me curiously, smiled, and said, 'We do chips by the bag, not by the number.' So, I simply asked, 'How many bags would I have to buy to get 51 chips?' He replied in a rather disgruntled manner, 'Look, we only have small, medium or large . . . so, which one do you want?' I thought about it for a second and replied, '51 *large* chips, please . . . or 102 *small* . . . if you've run out of the large ones that is . . . or 76-and-a-half medium if push comes to shove.' He stared at me blankly, scooped up a number of chips (without counting), wrapped them up, and said 'There you are, 51 large chips. That'll be £2.80.' I looked at him, a little disgruntled myself might I add, and said, 'Right-ho.'

"If you are in the business of chips, I believe it should be compulsory to have some experience with mathematics or numbers of some sort at least. It is not fish and *chip*! Chips are *plural*, more than one, and any more than one requires counting. I replied after some time, 'Well, now we've got that out of the way, can I have a fish?' This request seemed to exacerbate the entire queue of Frankey's Fish Bar, which was getting longer with every passing second. A few minutes of shouting and cursing transpired, and, in the end, I was given a fish free of charge with the condition that I left immediately. I was a bit surprised by all this hoo-ha, but I was determined it would not get me down. I replied, 'Okay, my strange fishy friends. Thank you for the service! Oh . . . and I'll just need another eight portions please . . . and may I ask if you do cocktail sausages?'

"I was just about to enquire whether they did pitted olives and, if so, whether they delivered, but I was swiftly nudged out of the shop, and before I knew it, a sign was placed in the shop window saying, 'Do not serve *any* amount of fish or chips to Mr Charles Dumbridge . . . as he is absolutely crackers .. and we don't sell those here.'"

Bertram Bloom

Bertram Bloom is a retired Headmaster, so, it's *Mr.* Bloom to you! He enjoys paneer and Sangria. He gains so much enjoyment from this rhyming couplet that he wishes to synthesise them as a customary meal somehow. I guess cheese and wine is a common enough pairing, so perhaps Mr. Bloom's proclivity is simply a Spanish Indian twist (a variation on a theme?). But who has paneer with sangria . . . really? One must adapt this to perhaps a paneer saag and a . . . (?). Mr. Bloom *always* mixes his orange juice with J.P. Chenet and a dash of brown sugar. Popular phrases of his include, "Here comes J.P., into the glass he goes," "It'll be a long night with J.P. this evening," "Where's the bloody J.P., Jeffrey?", "Oh Lord, J.P. me up!" and even sometimes "Jayyyyyyyyyyy Peeeeeeeeee".

Mr. Bloom has retained his pedagogical ways even to this day, asking the other Gentlemen's Club members whether they need to visit "Mrs. Murphy" before they embark on any club outings and correcting them on their misuses of grammar: "It's to *whom*, Clarence not to *who*." Mr. Bloom wrote a report on Cecil's first day at the Club, including general behaviour, skills he might add to the group, and overall performance. He also added a 'Comments' section, which could be completed by any of the members.

It remained empty for a few days before Cecil eloquently wrote "SOD OFF" (capitalized and ginormous for effect).

One Sunday at the club the topic of animals came up and Mr. Bloom (along with J.P.) had a few salient things to say on the subject:

...

"I have no problems with animals *generally*, it's when they all get turned into different groups and species and things. I mean, it's common knowledge that cats are just baby tigers, and ducks just look like birds slowly drowning. Who cares what *types* of dinosaurs there were, they should all just be bunched together as 'bloody terrifying'! Llama's look like camels but without the humps, as far as I'm concerned rats and mice are the same (I can never tell the difference). Flamingos look like bloody big birds with one leg, spiders look like tiny black crabs who enjoy the insides of cupboards, elephants look like giraffes who have spent too much time in London and are sexually impotent, dolphins are just clever sharks, all those small insect things, well they can just be grouped as annoying. Frogs and toads are two sides of the same amphibian coin, monkeys are just smaller bears that attended dance school. Rabbits, hares, ferrets, squirrels . . . I call them small fuzzy things. I mean, in a sense *they* (animals) have all got eyes, ears, noses, and mouths, just arranged differently. It's like notes in different pieces of music, the same just in a different order. Don't get me started on snakes, just large worms. Starfish? Just squishy normal fish that have been shaped by those pastry cutter things. Bats? Night-time giant butterflies. Octopi? Big underwater spiders (which, as we have established, are basically crabs, which, in turn, are basically sideways lobsters). Sleuths = monkeys with long fingernails (and koala bear faces). Fishes = things that go with chips. Alligators and crocodiles are just cubist versions of seals (with huge choppers!). If they have wings, they're birds (just with slightly different bits *between* the wings). Giraffes? Loch Ness Monster in leopard skin. Baboons are just one letter away from being bassoons . . . "

...

37

This went on for some considerable time until Mr. Bloom's bottle of J.P. was empty (he thought that maybe there was an invisible glass stuck somewhere at the bottom, which he attempted to shake out desperately but to no avail). He came to some roundabout conclusion before passing into a deep sleep. It went something like this:

...

"So . . . then we come to the human, man, person. But that silly billy is just a less hairy ape (apart from the case of Victor obviously). And the apes come from monkeys and the monkeys come from all the other fuzzy things. And the fuzzy things come from the weird non-fuzzy things. So, we all come from other things . . . even donkeys . . . especially Clarence . . . he's a donkey . . .

. . . J.P . . . ."

Henry Calming

THE LAST FEW DAYS at the Nettleham Gentlemen's Club have been so utterly perfect that neither a poet nor artist could add any more beauty to them. The slow fall and steady distribution of cherry blossoms, gradually moving easterly by the summer breeze as if pulled by some unknown force, residing neatly on the edges of pavements. The smell of freshly cut grass originating from the Nettleham F.C football pitch. The colour and taste of Kalamata olives mixed with broken feta cheese prepared and brought outside by Rebecca Bramble just after 5:00 p.m. The cacophony of laughter that each Gentlemen's club member produces, slightly different yet in complete harmony with each other, bouncing and reflecting off our bodies like the silhouettes of splashes and light waves perceived in indoor swimming pools. Nothing is for show and nothing is for sale. The setting is as modest as a piece of used chewing gum underneath a school desk.

Henry Calming is interested in absolutely nothing. He stops the other Nettleham Gentlemen's Club members when they are talking about the news, dismissing it as "only images and words on a television screen." He excuses himself at exactly 10:00 p.m. every night to go for a walk. When confronted on this routine he simply answers: "To see if everything is in the same place as it was this afternoon." He is always the first to get to the Pavilion in the mornings and shuffles the cards for us in advance for our first game of rummy. He has had no hobbies and does not wish to waste time on them in the future. He is always reluctant to do anything other than play cards and is one of the few members of the club that likes to indulge in something alcoholic before noon. Never married, never divorced, never interested. His mother was a professional concert singer and whenever he has 'three of a kind' he blasts into a reprise of one of her songs before shortly realising he has become the centre of attention, subsequently recoiling into a gentle cough or a sip of his drink.

He prefers an older currency than that used at present and remembers when chocolate bars were wrapped in paper and not plastic. He has a photograph of himself at three years old alongside his mother and father, in the bottom flap of his wallet. They are at the beach. His father is sporting a blue and white striped bathing suit whilst his mother is in all black, tilting a black sun hat. At three years of age Henry looks as lost and unsure of the world as he does now.

Henry remembers breaking toffee with a hammer and being terrified of Punch and Judy shows. He remembers hearing about the last brick that completed the Empire State Building and the first time he saw Donald Duck on the big screen.

Every time anyone mentions the beach to him, he thinks of his mother and father, how they separated, his journeys on the train between both of their houses, the Golden Age of the dining car yet having lumps in his throat due to his parents separation.

Maybe Henry Calming doesn't have to be interested in anything. Maybe too many interesting things have happened *to* him. Either way, Henry will always take his 10:00 p.m. walks, he will always tidy up after himself, he will always prefer his steak medium rare, he will always find excuses not to go to the beach and he will always commemorate his mother, without even knowing it, when he triumphs at card games. Little did Henry know that his father also used to take late night walks . . . and he even enjoyed a tipple before midday.

Not every Nettleham Gentlemen's Club member rejoices in the stupidity and humour of their actions. Not all members can muster the strength to affirm life eternally as Sydney does or Charles for that matter. Yet Henry is forever grateful and forever calm. Henry is content not to be interested, not to be bombarded from every angle by what the rest of the world is doing, its existential quandaries, its political representations, the new piece of technology that came out that day. In his very own words, "Just pour me a drink, deal the cards, and give me a window seat."

QUENTIN GREEN

"Whatever time I set my alarm for it always – and without fail – comes on at 4:00 AM in the morning! I don't dare get a new one because it might do the same but wake me up even earlier! The fire alarm always bleeps at me in the night, forever pestering me. Sometimes I get up on my bed and whisper to it gently, 'There is and will never be a fire in this bedroom . . . please, stop, fussing!' (Unless Victor makes one of his infamous bacon sandwiches in here.) The wallpaper needs de-creasing; it has all these lines and patterns on it, looks like Van Gogh brail for blind people. Why is it that carpets are always brown or grey? Is it because if someone spills wine, it can be easily camouflaged by this murky colour? I don't tend to drink in my bedroom, I drink in the study, and the carpet in there is also a kind of brownish cream (thank God)."

The Pavilion is also decked in this obscene colour, but it is always tidy (God bless Henry!) but also always stinks of Shropshire Blue and Celtic Gold . . . and cocktail sausages (God bless Victor and Clarence . . . in a way). I'm sure Bertram by now has written up an inventory classifying all the pieces of furniture and their subsequent damages (God bless Mr. Bloom!).

I do like to smoke in the bath though, it reminds me of a film I once saw. I'm unsure of what day it is but the Club will always have a spare newspaper knocking about to remind me. I like to do the crossword; it shows that I have accomplished something in the day. The trick is to inadvertently ask questions to the rest of the Club that pertains to the questions in the crossword. "Sydney, you make model aeroplanes, don't you? And did you ever come across Billy's Bomber? And that was a nickname for which aircraft again?"

When was the last time you ate mackerel? I mean, lovely grilled mackerel in the morning oozing with butter? It's already a good day if you've had mackerel and butter on toast! People worry too much. My mother always used to say "You can't change the world, but you can always change your attitude." My attitude is mackereley . . . and a cup of black coffee works wonders with it. I don't have a kettle you see. I boil the water and place it into a cafetiere, much nicer that way. You've got to spend a bit of time with the good things in life. It's July yet I'm still in March on my wall calendar; it's just such a beautiful picture! Hundreds of matchstick men walk to work past the factories, the streetlamps look like black and yellow crucifixes, little grey dogs are running through the legs of a paperboy, and you can see a lonely church in the distance. I don't think my eyes are ready for July (. . . or April for that matter).

Some new houses have been built near the Old Brown Cow. There's a lot of racket going on, but the occupants seem nice. One even smiled and said hello when I passed him on my way to the Pavilion (it was a sort of hushed "hello" because he was trying to get his baby to sleep). Some of them have started putting numbers on their recycling bins. Us older Nettlehamites just *know* whose bins are whose. For example, mine has an immaculate lid with an easy flapping motion, Clarence's reeks of cheese, Charles's wheels are squeaky clean because he rarely puts it out (he doesn't know what it's *for*). Victor thinks if he puts *his* out, then he'll never get it back.

I do hope Rebecca makes her famous apple pie this afternoon. It's the 'pie' bit that's so alluring; how do boring apples turn into *that*? I sometimes think about pushing up my sleeves and getting in on all this cooking action; what *is* 'pastry' and where do all the crumbs come from? What is so bubbly and squeaky about 'bubble and squeak' and is the *toad* in the hole meant to be the sausage? (Bertram would have something to say about that.)"

Endnote

So, there you have it. Nothing special. If the nine members of The Nettleham Gentleman's Club are not dead already then . . . they'll be *hiding*. Hiding because they do not wish to show the world what they have made. In a universe full of turmoil and cynicism, this club has made what they have wanted out of life. It is not to everyone's taste of course, but it is unified and coherent, even in fits of joviality. If you wish to visit Mulsanne Park, you are more than welcome to but such a story depends on the people that were there at a specific point in time; to people that were further *welcomed* like myself.

Other than that, what's it all about, eh? We all read books; I've only read a few in all honesty – and why? To parade the cultural diamonds of our present civilisation. Well there's nothing of that here. To communicate profound and necessary truths? That's all been said and done, hasn't it? Have a drink, and don't get so terribly melancholic. That's an order! There are always people around the corner to distract you from absolute wretchedness. That's just what the Gentleman's Club members did for me! There may be gods and demons and politicians and poets, but all of them (yes all of them) must put their socks on and tie their shoelaces. All of them get soaked when it's raining and all of them get tumper rumblings at around 4:00 p.m. (Maybe not Cecil . . . he'll be asleep by then.)

Perhaps the most pertinent question is: Why write a book about this kind of thing, these *kinds* of people? Documentation for one thing; when the gods finally awake from their slumber and come see what all the fuss is about, when the aliens finally muster up enough courage to come visit, it will be *these* kinds of people, these kinds of *gentlemen* that will appear the most fascinating. Zeus won't have time to evaluate the world *at large*; he'll get too caught up in the intricate mechanisms of a wristwatch or the taste of a perfectly poached egg. And when the time comes to *get on with the task in hand*, Bertram will pour Zeus a glass of J.P. or Victor will pass him a gin rickey and he'll graciously accept. Three glasses down and he'll be an official member of the Club . . . and officially . . . tipsy.

For better or for worse I'll be doing the same . . . but with them in spirit and not in company.

I have always wished to write about things that should never have been written; things not worth writing about. I have always preferred the gaps between the words, what was left unsaid. And so, I leave you with my latest book, so much silence and confusion, but so much peace and endlessness. Sometimes it is so beautiful to have *forgotten* what one wanted to say.